The Mystery of the One-Armed Man

A Captain Finn Treasure Mystery

LIZ DODWELL

Liz Dodwell

**The Mystery of the One-Armed Man: A Captain Finn Treasure
Mystery**
Copyright © 2014 by Liz Dodwell
www.lizdodwell.com

ISBN-10: 1939860091
ISBN-13: 978-1-939860-09-5

Published by Mix Books, LLC

Table of Contents

Liz Dodwell

For Alex
The future starts today

Forward

Single up on the lines and tell 'em below
To stand by the motors, we're ready to go
Put air on the whistle then give it a yank
Let go of all line and haul in the plank

There's nothing like a little nautical ditty or a good mystery book to get you in a treasure hunting mood. I've been in pursuit of Sunken Treasure for over 40 years. Much of the travel time is spent reading, and I believe I have read (maybe) all of the treasure novels, and most of the mystery books. I am proud to say I count among my friends the great, though sadly late, writer and explorer Sir Arthur C. Clarke, and novelist and marine archaeologist, Clive Cussler. I did much of the research for Robert Kurson's (of *Shadow Divers* fame) new novel, and have a new acquaintance in Randy Wayne White. I have written many articles about Sunken Treasure and really appreciate it when someone with writing talent can create a great story around a real-life treasure mystery.

My friend, Liz Dodwell, has written such a story, and you are about to read it. Most people read for a while and then take a break. I did after reading the first four chapters, but the thought of "What Next" occupied my mind to the point where I stopped my daily tasks and picked up the manuscript again, and with Rum in hand, continued. In my mind I found myself second-guessing as I started turning the pages, but I have to admit, I did not see the end coming. I would like to give you a couple examples of this, but I don't want to tip you off. Instead I will let you get on with your own second-guessing.

I'm anticipating Captain Finn will lead us on many adventures. I hope so, because I somehow feel a kinship with him. And so "For Treasure and Pleasure" here comes the first Captain Finn treasure mystery, *The Mystery of the One-Armed Man*.

Captain Carl Fismer
Key Largo

ONE

I felt it more than I heard anything. Just a slight rocking of the boat and a faint thudding, not rhythmic but spastic almost. We were at a private dock at the home of one of our sponsors on Sarasota Bay in Florida. The location gave us easy access through Big Sarasota Pass out to the "Slaver" site in the Gulf of Mexico. And it was free; a huge bonus for cash-strapped treasure hunters like us.

Anyway, back to the noise. Usually I can sleep through anything. Years in the foster care system with a bunch of rowdy kids, a summer sleeping rough on the streets of Philadelphia, and then a stint in the army, pretty much disciplines you to block out noise when sleep calls. This night, though, I was having flashbacks. Not severe, but I figured it was better to keep myself awake, so I was doing something I almost never do – giving myself a manicure. I'm not a girly girl. Given my background I don't think I ever learnt how to be, but sometimes I try. I'd picked out a color called Knockout Pout, and as I was applying the first coat *Time Voyager* shifted and I ended up with Knockout Pout everywhere but on my nails. Heavy weather was kicking up in the Gulf but it hadn't affected our sheltered berth, so I figured something might have hit us.

Just then I heard Finn come out of his cabin so I gave up on my beauty endeavors and opened my door.

"You felt it, too," he said.

"Something."

"Probably just a log but we'd better check."

I nodded and we headed up through the galley onto the aft deck. There was a quarter moon trying to smile through a cloud-covered sky. Stepping to the bulwarks we peered down into the water. It was black, though something was moving with enough frenzy to cast a few droplets of water over us.

"Shall I turn on the lights?"

Finn shook his head. "Let's not wake the neighbors yet. Go grab a flashlight."

By the time I got back with a rechargeable spotlight, Finn was waiting with a gaff in hand. I turned on the powerful halogen lamp and pointed it down.

"Ah, hell."

"Keep that light steady." Finn's voice was firm, calm. "I'm gonna drag it round to the transom, then you'll have to help me pull it in."

'It' was a body.

"I'm not touching it, and there are sharks as well. We need to call the cops and let them deal with this."

"Phill, that's a person down there and if we wait for the cops the body might sink and there'll be nothing here for them to deal with. I need your help -

now. Besides, that's only a small blacktip shark and he's more interested in all the fish round the body than in you."

Damn it. Finn is always so reasonable. Still, I wasn't going to stick my bare hands down there so I found a pair of heavy duty gloves and, as Finn began to raise the body up I managed to loop some line under the knees, and together we hauled the gruesome corpse onto the deck.

Bile stung in the back of my throat. I swallowed it down. The man, far from young, was naked except for a pair of boxer shorts that clung to chicken-thin legs. There was no aquatic detritus evident on the body and, though I'm certainly no expert, I was pretty certain he'd not been long in the water.

"Well, you were wrong about the shark." The man's right arm had been devoured all the way up to the shoulder.

Finn turned the light around and, crouching down, peered closely at the severed joint. "No." He looked up at me. "That's been hacked off with some sort of knife. And I would say very recently."

This time when the bile stung I hung over the gunwale and tossed last night's chicken chimichangas into the bay.

Liz Dodwell

TWO

It was mid-morning before the local constabulary were done. They'd called in the Coastguard as well, presumably to establish where the body might have entered the water. We were questioned several times over but the cops told us nothing, so we sat – me fidgeting like a cat with fleas, Finn patient – drinking too many cups of coffee that reminded me just how empty my stomach now was.

Perhaps this is a good time to tell you a little bit more about myself – and about Finn.

He's somewhere in his 60s I should guess, but he's never said and I've never asked. He has the face of a man who's really lived life: every line a testament to challenges and triumphs, heartaches and loves, risks and rewards. Whenever we're back in the Keys – the Florida Keys – he takes the time to dress up as a pirate captain and visit the kids in the children's hospital. Really, he's a complete softie. But he's tough, too. Hell, he's survived five types of cancer! It's amazing those light blue eyes are such beacons of life and laughter.

Finn's full name is Rex Finsmer but everyone calls him Captain Finn, or just plain Finn. For most of his life he's been a shipwreck treasure hunter; worked with some of the best, too. Now, he *is* one of the best. Two years ago when he found me I was in a really bad place. I'm not going to tell you about that yet, it's another story for another time. Suffice it to say that Finn saved me. Now I live with him on the *Time Voyager* and, no... don't go getting any ideas. Our relationship is like mentor and protégée or guardian and ward.... or maybe Laurel and Hardy (Finn and Phill – sounds like a comic duo, doesn't it?). Truth to tell, I never knew my father and I doubt my mother knew who he was, either, so I pretend to myself that my father is someone just like Finn.

Oh, and my name is Phillida Jane Trent. Don't ask me why; I've always supposed it was a random name issued by the orphanage. Nobody ever calls me Phillida or Liddy or anything cute. It's Phill, and I guess that's OK with me because there's really nothing about me that you could call cute. My hair is dirty blonde from being out in the sun, I'm exactly six foot tall and I rarely date. Guys seem to be intimidated by me. It used to bother me and I'd try and act feminine but Finn says to be myself, it's just going to take more of a man to be with me.

OK, back to the body.... or not. That seemed to be the end of it, though the police came by one more time to ask the same questions yet again. Other than that, we were in Sarasota for just two more days, re-stocking, doing some maintenance on the boat, and Finn had a presentation scheduled at the yacht club. That's where I come in. One of my jobs is to arrange talks where Finn can put on his show (I call it a show because he'll have everyone laughing one minute and on the edge of their seats the next). We bring artifacts to sell, and hope to find one or two people willing to sponsor a part of the adventure. Treasure hunting is expensive business. From the research, the boat, the maintenance, the equipment, the fuel, the time.... Most treasure hunters barely have enough to feed themselves. Over the years, Finn has been very successful, but expenses always seem to outweigh income.

Right now we were plotting a grid in the Gulf looking for a wreck that Finn believed was a slave ship. Slavers brought their live cargoes into New Orleans, and often left with gold and silver and other treasures from the sale. Working the grid was time-consuming and boring. Two other divers, Enos Donnell and Jafet Quintana regularly worked with us when we were in the Sarasota area and we all took turns in front of a small screen looking at pictures of the ocean floor created by side-scan sonar.

We'd been out almost two weeks when the weather turned against us. It was late August and reports were coming in that Hurricane Gisbert could be heading our way. You don't mess with hurricanes, at least Finn doesn't. He lost two boats in a hurricane a few years ago. So we high-tailed it back to Sarasota safety and hoped we wouldn't have to waste too many days at dock.

The first morning back I was fixing breakfast. Shrimp was on the counter waiting for a handout. Oh, yeah: Shrimp is our boat-cat. We were grilling shrimp when berthed at Stock Island in the Keys one day and this really skinny, mangy little calico cat turned up. We tried to coax her onboard and she'd tippy-toe close then get too nervous and dart off again. Finally, Finn grabbed a raw shrimp, held it out and said, "shrimp?" Well, that did it. She came right up and took the shrimp out of his hand. We tried different names with her but she'd completely ignore us. 'Shrimp' got her attention every time, though, so the name stuck.

Where was I...? Right, I was cooking breakfast while Finn was looking over the sonar images we'd taken, when we heard a voice call, "Ahoy, there." We looked at each other.

"Are we expecting anyone?"

I shrugged. "Not that I know of."

"Ahoy!" The caller was persistent.

Pointedly I looked at the pan of eggs I was scrambling. Finn took the hint.

"OK, I'll go."

I heard him call out 'Ahoy' as he went on deck.

"Permission to come aboard?"

"Absolutely, my dear. Let me help you."

My dear? To hell with the eggs. Who was this? I turned off the cooktop and followed Finn's footsteps in time to see him steadying a young woman as she stepped over the gunwale. She was my complete opposite: daintily feminine in floral culottes and a simple white top, with exotic features and sleek, dark hair.

"Are you Captain Finsmer?" Even her voice was soft and sweet.

"That's me."

"I'm Alana Azevedo and I'm hoping you can help me."

That's all it took. Finn never could turn down a damsel in distress - especially a pretty one. He ushered her into the salon, which is really just an extension of the galley, and offered her a seat on the L-shaped settee. I followed, making a point to ignore Shrimp who was chomping on the now-congealing mess that was meant to be breakfast.

Finn settled across from our guest and I scooched in next to him. He offered her some coffee – actually, he offered me to make some coffee – but she declined anyway.

"What can I do for you, Miss Azevedo?"

"Alana, please." She hesitated, then looked down, her hair curtaining across her face. Her shoulders shook just a little and I realized she was crying. Instinctively, I leaned forward to offer comfort but Finn deterred me with a shake of his head. In a moment, she had collected her wits again and looked up, unconsciously pushing her hair behind her ear.

"You found my grandfather not long ago."

Grandfather? I was confused. Then realization struck and the specter of the grizzly, one-armed body

15

turned my gut upside down all over again. Horrified, I looked at the young woman and hoped to god she hadn't had to see that for herself.

"I'm sorry," Finn said. It wasn't much but he had the ability to convey a whole lot of meaning in those two words. "Now, tell us why you're here."

Bit by bit, Alana told her story. She was Brazilian; her parents still lived in the Amazonas capital city of Manaus, in northern Brazil. She was their only child, and her mother was the only child of her now dead grandfather. She had never known her grandmother.

After earning her undergraduate degree in Brazil, she had secured a place at Columbia University Graduate School of Architecture in New York. Her grandfather had immediately bought an apartment where she could live and the family could stay on long-term visits.

"*Bought* an apartment?" That took some serious money in New York.

"My grandfather is very....*was*...very wealthy."

Alana continued that she was in her second year at Columbia. Her grandfather, whose name was Tobin Obotien, had come to spend the summer with her. He'd offered to take her away for a vacation – anywhere she wanted to go. Several of her friends had talked about Sarasota being a great city, so that's where she chose. "Just somewhere to relax on the beach, eat great food and look at gorgeous sunsets," she said, "and gear up for my third year."

Obotien had booked a two-bedroom, bay-view suite at the Ritz-Carlton and Alana had spent most of her days at the resort's Beach Club. Everything had been perfect; then something happened.

"We decided to have dinner at the Columbia Restaurant on St. Armand's Circle. Grandfather thought it would be a little bit of fun because I'm at Columbia U. We were seated inside at a window table and, even though it's hot, the tables on the sidewalk were full. Grandfather was just suggesting we visit the Ringling Museum of Art the next day, when his face turned ashen, his eyes opened wide and I swear he stopped breathing. At first I thought he might be choking or even having a stroke. His gaze was fixed on something outside and when I turned there was a man standing at a table who was staring back at us. Honestly, it was almost as if they'd each seen a ghost.

"Well, Grandfather suddenly came out of his daze and said he wasn't feeling well and that we had to leave immediately. He didn't even wait for the check: just threw money on the table and practically dragged me out of the place. There were taxis at the front door and he grabbed the first one and told the driver to just go; said he'd give him $100 to drive around for an hour – and that's what we did.

"I wanted Grandfather to go to the hospital but he absolutely refused, and wouldn't talk to me, either, except to say he'd feel better if we kept driving. It just didn't make sense, and when we got back to the hotel he said we would have to go back to New York the next day. I think he would have left right away, but by then I was frightened and insisted he lie down."

At this point Alana broke down. She seemed so brittle that a touch, or even a word, might cause her to shatter. I brought her a glass of water, then Finn and I waited her out.

"I'm sorry. I think I'm still in shock over this. None of it seems real."

"Take your time." Finn's voice was gentle. "When you're ready, tell us what happened after your grandfather lay down."

"That's just it. I don't know what happened! He lay on top of the bed and I thought he'd fallen asleep, so I took off his shoes and put a cover over him. Then I went to my own room and slept for a while. I woke at about two in the morning and tip-toed over to check on him – and he was gone! I freaked; called the front desk, checked the bar, the lounge, had hotel staff looking, even called the hospitals, but he was nowhere to be found. Finally, I called the police and filed a missing person report..... You know the rest."

"Alana," Finn leaned toward her, "what have you not told us?"

"Well," she drew the word out, "it was just so odd, but the man looking in the restaurant at us had only one arm."

THREE

Alana had been gone for a couple of hours, and since then Finn had been deep in thought. Several times I'd tried to interrupt him but he brushed me away. After we'd heard Alana's story, Finn had asked her again how she thought he could be of help to her.

"I want you to find out what happened and who did this," was her reply.

Bluntly, he'd stated that he hunted treasure, not criminals. Alana, however, had heard gossip that Finn had helped solve a crime or two – which is true – and added she had plenty of money to pay him. When Finn asked her why she thought he could do more than the police, her reply had surprised him.

"Because I think you care more."

At that he'd sent her away, with the promise that he'd make a decision by the afternoon. I didn't know what there was to think about: we needed the money! And to be honest, my heart went out to Alana who seemed so lost and alone. Finn was really good at solving puzzles and, if there was even a slight chance of him figuring this out, I thought he should try.

At last Finn surfaced. "Phill, there's something I need you to ask Alana: Was the guy at the restaurant missing his right or left arm?"

I punched the air and whooped. "We're taking the case!"

"I guess you should let Alana know and, Phill, ask her how I can talk to her mother, then find out who the lead detective is on this."

"Yes, sir!" I grabbed the phone and punched in the number Alana had given us. She answered almost immediately.

"Alana, you've got yourself a criminal hunter."

Turned out that Alana's mother, Luma, was already en route to Sarasota and would arrive the next day. Alana assured me that her mother would answer any questions Finn had. Meanwhile, she texted the detective's contact information to me and offered to let the police know we'd be in touch.

Having taken care of that, I returned to Finn. "OK, now what?"

"We need to find that one-armed man. Which arm is he missing, by the way?"

"Alana said the left one. Does it really matter, though?"

"It very well might."

Just then a text came into my phone. "From Alana," I informed Finn. "Detective Tanner is in charge of the case."

"See if you can get an appointment for me, then I want you to use your skills on the internet and find out everything you can about the Treasure of Lima."

"Ummm," the change of subject threw me, "are you planning a new expedition?"

"No."

"So what's the Treasure of Lima?"

"You'll find out when you do the research."

God, I hated it when Finn was cagey, but I knew better than to waste my effort trying to get anything more out of him. Just to be sure he knew I was irritated, though, I heaved a very audible sigh and rolled my eyes heavenward. Of course, it didn't have any impact on him so I gave up and reached for the phone again to call the detective.

Liz Dodwell

The Mystery of the One-Armed Man

FOUR

It was cocktail hour and I was making my version of a Fuzzy Pirate, with Blackbeard spiced rum, peach schnapps, blood orange bitters and fresh orange juice, and just a little sugar syrup. Yum!

I built the drinks over ice in two tall glasses and headed topside where Finn was sitting, eyes closed, with his feet propped up on an overturned bait bucket. Setting the cocktails on a folding table I pulled a sheaf of papers from my back pocket and smacked him with them. "Wake up! The bartender has poured, and I've got that information you wanted on the Lima loot."

"Alrighty, then." Finn took a generous sip. "That's good. And I wasn't asleep; I was thinking."

"Whatever you say." I couldn't keep the sarcasm from my voice.

"I guess you didn't get through to the detective."

"Not yet," I sat next to Finn, "but I left a message."

"OK, then give me what you've got."

"First off, accounts are varied about the Treasure of Lima, and a lot of people think its existence is hocus pocus. Assuming you're one of the believers, though, here's the dope.

"Pretty much everyone agrees the treasure was stolen from the Cathedral of Lima, in Peru, and included at least two, maybe four, solid gold statues encrusted with jewels. Some claim there's a written inventory that lists a whole collection of cloth of gold, jewelry, doubloons, chalices and such, in addition to the statues. The date of the theft is variously given as 1820, 1890 and, according to a couple of Australian newspapers, 1798.

"Majority opinion seems to be that the Spanish entrusted the treasure to William Thompson, captain of the British Brig, *Mary Dear*. Thompson was to transport it to Mexico for safekeeping from the wars of independence in South America. He and his crew couldn't resist the lure of riches and murdered the guards then set sail for Cocos Island – that's off the coast of Costa Rica – where they buried the treasure."

I paused for a quick sip of my drink before continuing.

"There's a different version of what happened to the treasure that states a pirate, Benito Bonito – otherwise known as 'Bloody Sword' - had it. Supposedly, he concealed the booty in a cave near Queenscliff, in the state of Victoria, Australia, but blew up the entrance when he realized a British man o' war was waiting for him in Port Phillip Bay.

"Over the years, both Queenscliff and Cocos Island have been searched by treasure hunters; all to no avail. Cocos is now a UNESCO world heritage site, so anything buried there is going to stay buried because digging is no longer allowed.

"A 1937 article in the Sydney Morning Herald reports that two jewel-encrusted gold statues were found in a 58 foot shaft in the Queenscliff caves by a diviner, of all things, but the shaft was closed for fear of subsidence before the relics were recovered. A later article on June 14, 1953, claims that a vacationer found an 18th century Spanish silver coin near the caves.

"Are you following this, so far?"

Finn nodded. "I've heard some of it before, but I suspect you have a few more morsels of interest to feed me."

"Nothing definite. Just some other odd tidbits."

"Go on, then."

"Well, first off, I couldn't find anything to confirm there ever was a 'Treasure of Lima,' or any ships fleeing Lima with treasure. However, according to one article, the Peruvian Colonial Archives were sold off in 1870. If that's true, then any reports would have disappeared.

"Then there's another character mentioned from time to time, who is sometimes called 'Stingaree Jack.' He might have been a cabin boy on Bonito's ship. At any rate, it's said he escaped the pirates, recovered some of the treasure, then hid it elsewhere.

"The last oddity is that Benito Bonito might have been Captain Thompson's mate, though other reports say it was a man named Chapelle. And that's it."

"Good job, Phill," Finn stroked his neatly trimmed beard and looked thoughtful, "that's a lot of information."

I shrugged my shoulders. "I'm damned if I see how it helps us figure out who killed Obotien."

"Oh, it does. It does."

"Are you going to spill? Or just leave me hanging?" Now I was irritable.

"We'll go over it later. Right now, you need to take those notes away and make three more Fuzzy Pirates."

"Three? Just how much of an alcohol fix do you need?"

Finn jerked his head toward the walkway. "We're about to have company."

FIVE

When I came back on deck with a tray of drinks, a woman was seated in my chair.

"Phill," Finn said, "this is detective Dixie Tanner. She's in charge of the Obotien investigation."

I figured detective Tanner must be in her fifties, but the lady was seriously in shape. Not many women that age can get away with a sleeveless, form-fitting dress. There were no jiggling biceps, her stomach was flat, and long, shapely legs were stretched out in front of her. She was even wearing heels, for Pete's sake. What kind of detective dresses like that?

"Call me Dixie," she said, "and I'm here informally." She must have noticed the way I looked at her clothing.

"Uh, hi. It should be OK for you to drink this, then?"

"This is?"

Finn broke in as I pulled up another chair. "Phill likes to create cocktails. Try it."

The lady took a tentative sip. "Wow. This is really delicious. I'm usually a dull vodka tonic; I might have to get more adventurous from now on. Thanks." She turned a full-on smile at me and I began to think she was pretty OK.

We all exchanged a few pleasantries about adult beverages and how our dock was well-sheltered from the still-rough Gulf waters before Dixie got down to the reason for her visit.

"Alana Azevedo told me she's hired you to look into her grandfather's death. She also said she'd like me to share information with you….. That's not likely to happen."

Finn said nothing; I figured I didn't like Dixie so much, after all.

"We're not in the habit of sharing information from an ongoing investigation with anyone, let alone someone who's not even a licensed investigator. Obviously, I can't prevent Ms. Azevedo from passing along things she may become privy to, but my Chief really wants to keep this thing under wraps. The town doesn't need a panic over a shark attack."

Shark attack? Did the police really believe that?

"Dixie, Dixie." Finn was shaking his head. "We both know this was no shark attack. And though you didn't say so, you're a *homicide* detective. You wouldn't be running a shark attack investigation."

She had the good grace to look a little uncomfortable as Finn continued.

"Here's what I think happened. Someone hacked off the man's arm, probably while he was still alive. That means there was likely to be an accomplice or two, because they'd need to hold Obotien down. To get rid of the body they went out into the Gulf. No doubt they planned to go a few miles out but the seas were really rough so they probably had to ditch the body quickly and get back into the relative safety of the bay. The flood tide through Big Sarasota Pass began that night at about 10.30pm, which means they were most likely out there after that time. And the tide was especially strong. My guess is the body was swept into the bay and ended up against my boat."

By now Dixie and Finn were locked in an eye fight; each holding the other's gaze and neither willing to give. I knew how this would end, though, and sure enough, Dixie finally looked down.

"Alright, Finn. I won't pretend this isn't murder. But why do you say Obotien was still alive?"

"The cuts were very jagged and you might assume a blunt knife was used. When I looked closer I could tell the knife was fairly sharp, so the jagged effect had to be because Obotien was struggling."

The detective ran her hands down her thighs as if smoothing out her dress. Then she uncrossed and re-crossed her legs. It seemed she was playing for a little time.

"You didn't hear this from me." She looked at Finn and glanced over to me. "Your conclusions agree with ours…. and Obotien drowned – he didn't bleed out. Beyond that, however, we've got nothing. No idea why Obotien left the hotel or where he went. No murder weapon; no crime scene."

"So you're saying he was dumped in the water right after his arm was cut off?" This was grizzly but I couldn't help myself – I was fascinated.

"Maybe not. I doubt the killers would have tried this on the boat with the weather as it was; they could all have been tossed overboard. And sometimes blood vessels will close up as an automatic protective measure when a limb is severed. He could well have survived for an hour or so."

"I take it you're checking boats that left their moorings that night?" Finn asked.

"That's a dead end. Most people were too busy bracing for the storm. And if the boat came from a private dock – just like here – who would notice?"

"What about the other one-armed man?"

Dixie looked startled. "What man?"

So Finn told her about the man Alana saw at the Columbia Restaurant. Dixie seemed pretty miffed that Alana had not told the police about him, to which Finn suggested they had not asked the right questions.

The tension was rising again; time for me to jump in. "Another drink, anyone?"

Finn got the message. "Sure. Let's all have one. And what are you fixing for dinner?"

I glared at him. That wasn't quite the message I wanted to send. "Whatever take-out we order."

"Look," the detective rose. "I barged in on you. What say I go get pizza? I like mine with double cheese, pepperoni, Italian sausage and bacon if that suits you. Maybe a few cannolis, too?"

"Done," Finn said. And as she headed off I looked at him, "I like her."

SIX

It was 7am and I was on a mission. After we'd chowed down on pizza the night before and Detective Dixie had taken her leave, Finn announced that he needed me to do some surveillance.

"Surveil what?"

"Now that the good detective knows about our other one-armed man, it won't take her long to track him down. I'm betting that by tomorrow she'll be paying him a visit and you're going to be following behind."

"How am I supposed to do that?"

"You'll be waiting outside police headquarters. Get Enos and Jafet to help, and use two vehicles." Fortunately, we had the use of a car our sponsor kept at the house. "One of the guys will need to watch to see what car she drives away in, so find a picture of her to show them - there's bound to be something online. Just get me the man's address and don't," he really stressed the 'don't,' "do anything else. This guy could be very dangerous."

"If you think you're going to talk to him without me...."

"I'm not going to talk to him at all," Finn interrupted. "I only need his name. And I'm hoping that once we have his address you'll be able to find that out."

As usual, Finn was no more forthcoming, so I'd taken myself to bed. Now, here I was with Jafet, parked – unobtrusively, I hoped – near the police station. Enos had drawn the short straw and was hovering near the Courthouse Café. I was already on my second coffee and wondering what I was going to do if, or should I say when, I needed to hit the bathroom.

An hour later I needed to pee so bad my eyeballs were floating, and I was thinking I'd dash to the café to relieve myself and, as long as I was there, grab one of their amazing breakfast sandwiches, when my phone rang. It was Enos; Detective Dixie was on the move. She had another cop in the car with her and I followed them east along Fruitville Road until she pulled into a Dunkin' Donuts. The two of them went inside; I did a sharp turnaround and headed to a nearby store I knew would have a ladies' room. Meanwhile, I called Enos, who was in his old truck a few blocks behind, and told him to take over for a while.

It wasn't long before the detective and her compadre left the donut shop and headed north with Enos and me – much relieved - not far behind. We wove around a few streets: a walled development of mobile homes came up on our right – or modular homes, I guess I should say – and Dixie turned into the entrance. I kept driving, glancing in as I passed. It was a gated community with a guardhouse. *Aw jeez. Now what was I going to do?* The police vehicle was quickly allowed in and I pulled to the side of the road, wondering what to do.

Just then, a van pulled up to the gate. Along the sides were signs that read, 'Jim Will Fix It. No job too small,' and an idea popped into my head. I turned to Jafet.

"Quick. Get into Enos' truck and follow that van as if you're with Jim the fixit man. Pretend you can't speak much English. They might just let you in."

Fortunately, Jafet was a quick study. He ran over to the truck and swapped places with Enos and managed to pull up to the guardhouse moments after the van pulled away. Enos joined me in the car and we could see Jafet gesticulating wildly. The guard shook his head several times, Jafet got more animated and, finally, the gate opened and we were in. Enos and I high-fived, then I got on the phone to Jafet.

"Just find the detective's car, get the address, then get back out here."

The community was pretty small; it only took a few minutes and Jafet rang back. "OK, it's 1718 Pawpaw Place."

"Got it. Let's hope it's the one armed man's home, because I don't think we can do this all day."

"It is."

"How do you know?"

"I'm looking at him."

I squeaked. "Jafet, you can't be seen. Drive away."

"Don't sweat it. The cops are at the front door with their backs to me, and if anyone even notices me they'll think I'm just another one of the Mexican workers around the place."

I was only slightly mollified. "Alright, but we've got what we need. Let's go."

"On my way."

We were sitting round the galley table, sipping on Florida Cracker Ale from Cigar City Brewery as Jafet recounted his adventure to Finn. OK, it was only 10.30 in the morning and some of you probably think that's a little early for beer, but we *had* been up since five. Anyway, for the heck of it Jafet had taken some cell phone pictures. The first was of the home; a neat-looking place with a cheerful coat of blue paint. According to Jafet, the neighborhood in general had a well-cared-for appearance. The next picture showed the front door, and we could just make out the one-armed man as he spoke to Dixie. Then there was a close-up of the man's face. Though it was a bit blurry, it was the face of a man as old as Obotien. *Weird.* Now we had two one-armed octogenarians.

The guys didn't hang around, and as soon as they left, Finn asked me to research the address. It only took a few minutes of online browsing to find a name – actually two - using the Sarasota County Property Appraiser's website: Rodrick and Elise Hardie. They'd owned the home for 15 years. Of course, the one-armed man could be a renter, but Finn seemed pretty certain that Rodrick was both the owner and, hence, Mr. One-arm.

"Now that we have a name," Finn said, "there's something else I want you to search for."

Less than an hour later I handed Finn the results of my efforts. "This is pretty bizarre, to say the least. There are five names there, but I don't get where Obotien fits in."

Finn cast his eye over the papers and gave a satisfied grunt.

"You know what this is about, don't you?" I persisted.

"I've a pretty good idea." Then he stabbed his finger on the papers. "This is about greed and retribution. Too many people have suffered, directly and indirectly, and it's time it stopped."

Liz Dodwell

SEVEN

While the guys and I had been surveilling, Alana had called Finn. Her mother was in Sarasota and anxious to get together, so plans had been made to meet later at the Ritz.

"Why don't we leave now and take a detour for lunch at the Linger Lodge?" Finn stretched his arms over his head.

"Fine by me. That's a pretty long detour, though."

"I can use the time to get my thoughts in order before the meeting."

"And I can use the time to decide whether I want alligator bites or catfish nuggets." I was happy, but then it doesn't take much.

We arrived at the Ritz around four. Alana was waiting in the lobby for us. She looked fragile and fatigued; her eyes rimmed in bruise-colored flesh.

"Mother had to identify my grandfather today. We went together but I couldn't look. It was quite a shock for her so she's been lying down. She'll be ready for you by the time we get to the room, though."

We murmured our sympathy as Alana ushered us to the elevator and we glided upward.

Stepping into the suite was a moment of culture shock for me. I'd never experienced anything so utterly sumptuous. Everything was in muted shades of coral and pistachio with the blue of the bay as its backdrop. It was bigger than most apartments I'd been in, with a separate dining room and bedrooms and full-length balcony. We settled ourselves into the parlor. Alana offered drinks, which we declined, then the bedroom door opened and Luma Azevedo appeared.

It was quite apparent where Alana got her beauty. Unlike her daughter, however, Mrs. Azevedo was completely composed. Whatever her emotions at this time, she kept them not just restrained, but totally out of sight.

Finn and I both rose as she entered. I let Finn step forward to offer his hand, which she took as she accepted his condolences. Finn introduced me and the hand I clasped was cool, and the grip confident. It was all a bit formal and I felt rather awkward. Finn, as always, was quite at ease.

"Mrs. Azevedo….," she didn't even suggest first name terms, "…there are many pieces to this puzzle that span many years and three continents. To complete the puzzle there are several questions I would like to ask you."

"Captain Finsmer, I appreciate you coming straight to the point and I'm heartened you may be close to bringing sense to this dreadful deed. I assure you, I will answer all your questions as best I can."

"Thank you. There is something I must say first, though. The truth of this matter may be very unpleasant for you to hear. If you fear your memories may be destroyed, please say so now, and the knowledge I have of this affair will never be spoken of by me," he nodded slightly in my direction, "or anyone else."

Alana gasped and her mouth went slack. Her mother barely registered a flicker of the eyelids.

"Captain, right now the only memory that is imprinted on my mind is that of my dead father's body in the morgue. Your inference is that by some action of his own, he brought about his demise. I will tell you, that does not surprise me." At this, Alana seemed to shrink into the chair. "Though we had a close relationship, my father would never talk about his life before coming to Brazil….. but there were rumors."

She reached over and began stroking her daughter's hand. "I'm sorry, darling. He was wonderful to you as a grandfather, but I hope I've raised you to understand that truth is strength, and we should always face it."

Then to Finn, "Captain, I am more fearful of not knowing the truth, so please, ask me your questions."

Leaning toward her, Finn spoke.

"Have you ever heard any of these names? Gilbert Stenger, Rodrick Hardie, Joeri Baanders, Rowan Payton or Cyril St. Martin."

"Say them again, please."

Slowly, Finn repeated the names and Mrs. Azevedo shook her head. "I don't recognize any of them."

"That's OK. Can you tell me, what nationality was your father?"

"His nationality now is Brazilian. When I was a child, there was talk in the household that he was from America, but as I said before, the past was not discussed."

"Perhaps you can tell me the year he moved to Brazil."

Closing her eyes, she thought for a while. "It must have been around 1970, though I can't be sure. I was born in 1972 and I do know my parents had been married only a year at that time. It's my belief my father had not been long in the country when he married my mother. Is this of any help at all?"

"It's all good. I know the questions must seem random; bear with me."

"Of course, Captain."

Clearing his throat, Finn continued. "Do you have any idea what your father's profession was before Brazil?"

"Before he came to Brazil? Well, for my whole life he was in investments. I suppose I just assumed he'd always done that. There is something, though. I wonder if he might have done something in the medical field."

"Why is that?"

"My mother died giving birth to me. My nanny was the nurse who was there when I was born. She told me once how my father fought to help save my mother's life, giving instructions to the doctor and staff in the way only someone with medical knowledge could. She also said my father had been deeply in love with my mother and was devastated by her loss."

For the first time, the lady showed some emotion as her eyes clouded with tears. Finn gave her a little while to compose herself, then went on.

"One last question. Was your father right or left-handed?"

"He was left-handed."

"Thank you, Mrs. Azevedo. That's all."

"Is there anything more you can tell me now?"

"I need to speak with Detective Tanner. But I believe that very soon I will be able to give you the full story."

With that, Finn rose. I closed the pad in which I'd been scribbling notes and followed suit. We left the ladies to their grief and headed back to the lobby.

"I need to run to the bathroom," I said as we exited the elevator.

"Why didn't you go upstairs?"

"It just seemed awkward." I help up my hands in an 'I don't know' gesture. "I won't be long."

"I'll get the car and meet you out front," Finn called after me as I dashed off.

To me, the bathroom was like a lady's boudoir, and I must admit I lingered on one of the plush stools so I could spritz with the complimentary cologne and massage my hands with cucumber melon lotion. I was beginning to feel quite zen, but the mood was broken when a couple of women came in and gave me and my thrift-store couture a down-the-nose look; so I exited.

I didn't pay any attention to the old guy hovering in the hall. I figured he was waiting for one of the women 'til he stepped toward me and pressed something hard and cold into my side.

"That's a 9mm handgun you're feeling, and I'm more than willing to use it."

Shit! Mr. One-arm. Frantically, I looked around for help.

"Don't even think of doing anything. If you run, I'll shoot. Maybe I'll miss you but what's to say a stray bullet won't hit someone else. Like those kids over there." Three children with their parents were looking in the window of one of the boutiques. My knees felt weak.

"Now, we're going to walk casually out the back door, like we belong together." He dug the pistol in harder, which made 'casual' a little tricky for me, especially as we were going in the opposite direction to Finn.

For an old guy missing a limb, Hardie (I was assuming that's who it was) was surprisingly spry. He steered me round the back of the hotel, past the pool area until we eventually ended up in a neighboring strip mall where he shoved me against a dark blue cargo van. He'd obviously planned this out, but how did he know Finn and I would be at the Ritz? For that matter, how did he even know about us? Unless it wasn't us he was after. That must be it. He wanted Alana or her mother.

I tried to act dumb, which isn't that much of a reach, by babbling that he must have made a mistake. "If you think you'll get a ransom for me, I'm poor. I know I was at the Ritz but that was just to visit someone, and they won't pay anything for me – they only just met me."

It wasn't working. "Reach under the wheel-well there and you'll find a magnetic key holder," he snarled.

I did as instructed and proceeded to unlock the vehicle.

"Get in the side and grab one of those zip ties," they were lying by the door, "and tie your ankle to the passenger seat frame." This was just getting better and better. By the time we were done I was trussed up on the cold metal floor like a turkey with nowhere to go but the Thanksgiving table. Hardie also took my notepad and cell phone, tossing the phone in a nearby trash can. The book he placed on the front seat without looking at it, ten drove away.

We probably drove for about an hour. From my lowly position I had only a few inches of vision out the top of the driver's side window. At first we passed buildings, then it became trees or open sky, but I could tell from the way the sun came into the van that we were heading east, maybe to Arcadia. I kept trying to talk to Hardie, asking him what he wanted with me, telling him about me – you know, the old bonding theory – begging him to tell me about himself. No matter; he spoke only once and his words were "Shut it!"

EIGHT

The last part of the journey was over rough road, which my butt didn't appreciate at all. And I was really getting scared. Wherever we were, it was off the beaten track. I knew Finn would be looking for me but Hardie wasn't going to make it easy.

When the van came to a stop, Hardie climbed out, shutting the door behind him. I heard faint voices. So he had an accomplice – or two. I strained to listen. The voices raised as if in argument but it was as unintelligible as a television on low in another room. Then it was quiet. Minutes later the side door slid open again. Hardie stood there; a second guy looking over his shoulder. I sniveled and whined, hoping if I appeared beaten they might drop their guard and give me a chance to do something. These guys were highly organized, though.

"I'm going to give you some pills." It was Hardie who spoke. "Take them nicely and it will be easier on you."

He reached in through the front passenger door and came back with a little plastic cup; the kind they use in hospitals. And, sure enough, there were some yellow pills in it. He held it up to my mouth and I instinctively jerked my head around, knocking cup and pills flying.

"I warned you."

He looked back at his cohort, "Ready?" Then he pulled something from his pocket and thrust it into my chest. I went rigid, as a bolt of pain shot through me. I knew I was being hit with a stun gun but everything other than my mind was paralyzed. As soon as Hardie released the gun, I crumpled, feeling weak as a new-born kitten. Next moment he had his hand on my face, forcing my mouth open while I was unable to resist. The second guy shoved something into my mouth and I felt liquid squirting down my throat. *What the hell? Did he only have one arm, too?* Although I was coming round quickly my automatic reaction was to swallow. I managed to lift my head as Hardie released me and his pal tossed aside a now-empty syringe plunger. With a satisfied grunt, Hardie closed the door.

My mind went into overdrive. What the hell had they given me? Whatever it was, I needed to get it out of my system. Leaning over I was able to get my fingers in the back of my mouth and force myself to gag. Aqueous fluid spewed over my feet. I tried a couple more times but didn't do much more than belch, so figured that was as good as it was going to get.

It was getting hot, too. I needed a plan, assuming of course that I didn't die of heat stroke first. Late afternoon in August the temperature was probably about 90, and the van was in the open with no apparent cloud cover. In only 30 minutes it could be well into the 120s inside. I looked around for anything that might be useful – nothing. I tried to make my hands small enough to slip through the ties – not even close. *How did Houdini do it?* I was beginning to feel really sleepy, whether from the drugs or rising heat I didn't know. *Stay awake, Phill. Think about an ice-cold beer or cool dip in a pool.* Instead, I sagged against the seat, my eyes heavy and my brain begging me to fall asleep.

Just as I was about to enter the land of nod there was a slight scraping at the side of the van and the door opened. Instantly, adrenaline coursed through my body and shoved aside some of the torpor. I willed myself to appear limp. I even had a moment of thankfulness for the heat, which had dried up my vomit, so there was little sign I was in anything but a state of inertia.

Hardie grabbed my hair and lifted my head. When he let go I allowed it to drop like a Raggedy Ann doll. Satisfied, Hardie cut the bonds that tied me to the seat, but left my wrists and ankles tied together. I allowed myself to flop over in such a way that my head hung out the door and I could get a peek outside. A four-wheel utility cart had been placed beside the van. He was going to drop me in it and drag me away. Well, it was time to quit spitting on the handle and get to hoeing.

As he pulled me through the door I swung my legs round and dropped to the ground then pushed upwards, swinging my fettered hands to his face and smashing his nose. Blood spurted everywhere. Hardie was taken completely by surprise, so I pressed the advantage by stabbing him in the throat with two fingers. I pulled back a little before contact; a part of me felt bad for beating up an old man even though he'd most likely killed already and might kill me. At any rate, he dropped to his knees, helpless, gagging for breath. It was then something hit me in the back of the head. I had a moment of comprehension before blackness took over and that was it.

At first I was vaguely aware of an insistent throbbing in my head. Somewhere there was a sort of ringing hum – then I realized it was in my ears. *I'd been knocked out.* At least my memory was intact but I was having difficulty shaking the fuzziness from my brain, and when I forced my eyes open I looked out on a gray haze. The ground where I lay was hard and cold. I needed to get up. A sense of urgency was setting in. I had no idea where Hardie and his pal were but they could return any minute and I didn't think that would be good news for me.

My wrists and ankles were still tied; my arms pulled behind my back. I managed to get to my knees and, as my vision cleared, look around. Where the hell was I? The floor was concrete, the walls white tile. At least, they'd been white once. Now they were cracked, chipped and stained – everything was stained. The room was almost square and across the ceiling were two rusty metal bars with equally rusted hooks suspended from them. A very faint and distasteful metallic odor was in the air. I couldn't quite place it but it turned my stomach.

OK, it was time to get out of here and, thankfully, I had an ace in the hole. I used to know a couple of Armenian brothers who ran a leatherworks shop. One of their specialty items was belts with hidden compartments cut in them to hide money. They'd given me a couple of them for doing some work. My belt held a folding ceramic razor knife. When people search you, even if they pat you down, they never think to look on the underside of a belt. The knife was hardly more than an inch and a half long, no good as a weapon, but you never knew when you might need a knife – like now. And it was super sharp.

The secret pocket was in the front of the belt, so I just needed to get my hands there. No problem, I was pretty limber. I could easily work my butt and legs through my fettered hands.

Not so. There was resistance as I tried to pull my arms under my rear. I looked up and behind. *Son of a ...* A rope was attached from my wrists to one of the hooks above me. Fear began to edge its way into my mind. I pushed it aside. *Focus, Phill.*

Alright. I can slide the belt around. I began to pull and almost immediately the loose end at the buckle caught on a belt loop. OK. The other way, then. It worked! I felt for the hidden zipper and carefully undid it. A wave of adrenalin surged through me as my fingers closed round my trusty little knife. I flicked it open and, with a little maneuvering was able to slice right through the ties without cutting my wrists open. It took barely a heartbeat more to slice through my other bonds and I was free. Well, partly. I still had to get out of the building.

The room wasn't that big. There was a single dark window in one wall. I crept to it and peered through. In the gloom I could make out an even smaller room than the one I was in, with a couple of boarded up windows, a door and some shelving that had partly collapsed. An old office, maybe? No sign of the two guys, thankfully.

In the corner was a single door. I put my ear to it and listened for a while. Nothing. Slowly I turned the handle and pushed. It wouldn't budge. On the far side of the room were large metal sliding doors. The kind you see at a loading dock. When I tried to pull them apart I could see through the open slit that they were padlocked shut with a fairly new-looking chain. Right then, back to the other door.

There was no lock on my side. It was either bolted from the inside or blocked with something. Oh, well. I'm a big strong girl, so I put my shoulder to it and gave it all I'd got and opened it maybe a quarter of an inch. Forget that. One of the one-arms could be back any minute with something more powerful than a stun gun. I had to move fast. The window it would have to be.

An old hook was obligingly lying at my feet. I picked it up. It looked as if it could stand some stress so I hefted it back and smashed it into the window. The glass shattered and I waited, hardly daring to breath, in case Hardie and buddy came running …or walking fast, or however old guys move. When I figured it was safe to breathe again, I took off my shirt, wrapped it round my arm and pushed the glass away so I could climb over the sill into the office. Heading to the door I prayed to all the gods that it be open. Tentatively I turned the handle and, hallelujah, the door opened easily.

Steady Phill. I had no idea what might be outside.

There was Hardie's van. No sign of any other vehicle or of the two men. A short distance away was the skeleton of a long metal building with twisted shelves and wire grid fencing. All around, the land was open; just a few trees here and there. I stepped outside, throwing my blouse behind me. It was embedded with shards of glass; no way could I wear it again, which really pissed me off because it was a Tahari and the only decent one I had.

I made a dash for the van, yanked at the door and damned if it didn't open. I scrambled in and locked the doors behind me, hoping against hope that the keys were in the ignition. They weren't, but there was the next best thing –Hardie's phone sitting on the console. Punching in Finn's number and hearing his voice was one of the best things that had happened to me for a long time.

"I don't know where I am."

"It's OK, we do."

"We?"

"I'm with Detective Tanner. We've been tracking the cell phone signal."

"Oh, good," I mumbled and promptly keeled over and passed out.

NINE

Time Voyager was bobbing gently at her berth. Six people were seated throughout the galley: Luma and Alana Azevedo, Detective Dixie, Enos, Jafet and, of course, Finn. I was serving my newest cocktail creation, for which I'd borrowed the pirate Benito Bonito's nickname - Bloody Sword. It was made with my own black pepper-infused vodka, celery salt, Worcestershire sauce, horseradish, pickle juice, olive juice, lemon juice and tomato juice. I rimmed the top of the glass with Old Bay seasoning and garnished with olives and a pickle slice. *Oh, yeah, that's what I like.*

My memories of the previous day were fuzzy. Finn had quickly become alarmed when I didn't appear and he couldn't reach me on my phone. He checked with the Azevedos to see if I was with them. A word from Mrs. A. immediately had the hotel staff asking questions, and it didn't take long to find a guest who'd noticed me and a one-armed man in the pool area. Of course, Finn realized it was Hardie so he called Dixie and urged her to put a trace on the man's phone.

Apparently, my prison had been the slaughterhouse on an old chicken farm – no wonder it smelled so off. When my rescuers arrived they found me still out cold. I was shipped to the hospital where it was discovered I'd been dosed with sleeping pills. There'd be no long-term effects. If I hadn't up-chucked, though, the doctor said I might have been in serious trouble. Hardie and his pal were picked up later at a Tampa hospital. After tying me up, Joeri Baanders – the pal – had taken a suffering Hardie to the emergency room and tried to convince the staff his smashed nose and bruised throat were the result of falling on his face.

Now Finn was about to explain to Alana and her mother what this was all about. He stood and cleared his throat and all eyes turned to him.

"You might think this story began just a few weeks ago, when the body of Tobin Obotien was found. In fact, it begins in 1968. Five men, Gilbert Stenger, Rodrick Hardie, Joeri Baanders, Rowan Payton and Cyril St. Martin went on a treasure hunt. Hardie, Baanders and Payton were experienced divers. St. Martin was a researcher and Stenger, the money man, a successful surgeon by profession.

"They were after the Treasure of Lima, a hoard of jewels, coins and artifacts worth upwards of $300 million in today's currency. It was reputed the treasure had been stolen from a Peruvian catholic church in 1820 by a British ship's captain and hidden on Cocos Island. Another story claimed the treasure had been in the possession of Benito Bonito, a pirate who brought the cache to Queenscliff, in south-eastern Australia.

"Cyril St. Martin's research concurred with that, except he believed Bonito did not hide the treasure in a cave at Queenscliff. His evidence suggested Bonito's ship wrecked with the treasure on board somewhere in the eastern part of the Bass Strait. So that's where the five men headed."

"Where exactly is the Bass Strait?" It was Enos asking.

"It runs from Melbourne to Tasmania, in south east Australia."

Finn took a sip of his drink before picking up his narrative.

"They were searching the Strait when they got caught in a sudden, and vicious, squall that knocked out their power and drove them further east and on to a tiny granite island. At first, they counted themselves lucky – they were all alive. Soon it became evident they were in serious trouble. Their boat had disintegrated on impact and there had been very little to salvage. The island was pretty much uninhabitable; not much more than smooth steep rock where only an occasional sea bird landed. And the waters were heavily shark infested. Worst of all, apparently they were nowhere near any shipping lanes.

"There were a couple of small caves where they managed to find some shelter. When it rained, water would pool in rock basins. They used their clothing to try and slap birds from the air and catch fish, but without much success, and they had to eat them raw. After a few weeks, it was evident they were starving to death.

"They had a meeting to decide what to do. The idea was put forward that one of them sacrifice himself for the good of the others."

"Oh, god." Alana held her hand over her mouth and turned an ugly shade of gray.

"I don't get it," Jafet, this time. "You mean like a sacrifice to the gods, or something?"

"No," Finn replied. "They were discussing cannibalism."

"Sweet Jesus."

"Let me go on," Finn said.

"Instead, they decided to each forfeit an arm – their non-dominant arm. They would have a lottery of some sort to figure who would go first, but it was agreed that Stenger be last. He was the surgeon after all and would need both hands to wield the only knife they had between them.

"Rodrick Hardie was the first to lose his arm. When the flesh was offered to Cyril St. Martin, he went completely crazy. He threw himself into the water and began to swim. He didn't make it very far before the sharks got him.

"Payton and Baanders both had their limbs removed, though Payton's wound became infected, and within a few days he was dead. That left only Stenger. Luckily for him, it was at that time they were discovered by a couple who had gone off course in their sailboat. They were able to radio for help and Stenger and the two others were saved."

Detective Dixie leaned forward, resting her arms on her knees. "You should all know that this information has been corroborated by Joeri Baanders. Rodrick Hardie is still under sedation at hospital. However, there's no reason to believe he won't confess."

"How did you figure it out, Captain?" Luma Azevedo asked.

"Treasure hunters are a small fraternity and I've heard pretty much every story there is out there."

"And Finn remembers everything," I put in.

"Most things," he corrected. "So when Alana told me about the one-armed man at the restaurant, and I considered his and Obotien's ages, I remembered hearing about the treasure hunters who were found with their arms cut off. That's why I asked Alana if her grandfather was right or left-handed. When she said left-handed I was pretty sure I was on track, because Obotien had his non-dominant arm cut off.

"Then I had Phill do some research and she found a newspaper article about the men, which listed their names. From there, it didn't take much to confirm that the man at the restaurant was Rodrick Hardie and it was a pretty fair guess that Tobin Obotien was, in fact, Gilbert Stenger. Now here's where some speculation comes in.

"I believe Stenger found the treasure, or part of it at least, on that barren island. Detective Tanner has people searching to see if there's any evidence Stenger went back to the island and I'm sure, in time, they will find something."

Here Dixie jumped in again. "We do know that Stenger disappeared soon after. It was thought he might have committed suicide but no body was ever found."

"So my father *was* a doctor," Luma Azevedo murmured almost to herself. More stridently she said, "You're saying he cheated those other men; kept the treasure to himself, and I was raised on money that was stolen from the church?"

"That's about it," Finn said. "And in case you haven't figured it out, the name Tobin Obotien is an anagram of Benito Bonito."

"I'll be damned," Enos shook his head. Beside her mother, Alana quietly cried.

"To continue." Finn cast his eye over the group and waited for them to settle back down.

"That brings us to the present day. Hardie and Obotien must have recognized each other at the restaurant. Although Obotien tried to cover his tracks to the Ritz, it's apparent that Hardie found him there. He must then have called Joeri Baanders. Australian by birth, Baanders moved to the US soon after the terrible incident. Maybe he planned to search for Stenger. At any rate, he now lives in Cape Coral, Florida and must have responded to Hardie's plea immediately.

"Detective Tanner and I believe that Hardie and Baanders coerced Obotien to leave his room by making threats against Alana. The front desk confirmed that a call was put through to the room and answered by Obotien."

Alana looked up quickly. "There *was* a call. Grandfather said it was confirming our wake-up call for the morning. Oh, God. This is all my fault. If I'd agreed to leave when he wanted to, he'd still be alive today."

Her mother wrapped her arms around her and for the first time looked helpless.

"Alana," Finn's voice was gentle, "once the others knew your grandfather was alive, they would never have stopped looking for him. You, your family, and who knows how many others might have been hurt."

"Like Phill," Alana said. "I am so, so sorry."

"It wasn't your fault," I stressed and Enos added, "Yeah, what was that all about?"

"Most likely, Hardie was staking out the Ritz planning to kidnap Alana and hold her for ransom. We think," he looked over at Dixie, "taking Phill was a crime of opportunity. Alana had been holed up in her room or was always with her mother. Remember, it's not easy for an 80-year-old handicapped man to kidnap someone."

"Hey," I couldn't let that go unchallenged. "He was an 80-year-old handicapped guy with a gun."

"I thought revenge was the motive here?" Jafet looked puzzled.

"The taste for revenge had more than four decades to fester. What's more, both men struggled financially all that time. Baanders wife refused to come to the US with him and he's had no contact with either of his two kids since then. Hardie never had children but stayed married to Elise. Now she's in a nursing home, which they can't afford. Obotien ruined their lives. It took a lot of hatred to do what they did."

We all fell silent. Mrs. Azevedo rose to her feet. "Captain, you did exactly what was asked of you. However much I wish the truth were different, I do thank you. Right now, I need to concentrate on my daughter..." her words dried up and it was obvious she was struggling to hold herself together.

No-one commented. None of us knew what to say, but Finn and Enos help Alana to her feet then escorted mother and daughter to the limo they had waiting for them. When they returned, Jafet asked, "Where did they kill him?"

Dixie answered. "Possibly at the old barn where Hardie took Phill. There's no blood evidence at his home and we still haven't found the boat they must have used."

"Do you think they sedated him first?"

"No!" Finn was emphatic. "I think they wanted him to suffer as much, or more, than they did."

With that, we all sat gloomily for a while and soon the guys drifted away, then Dixie got up.

"I'd better go. I have reports still to finish."

"OK, I'll see you tomorrow," Finn said. "Pick you up about seven?"

"Perfect," she smiled. Then left.

"Where are you going so early?" I hated not knowing everything that was going on.

"I'm not going anywhere in the morning. I'm taking Dixie to dinner in the evening."

"Oh." There was nothing more to say.

Liz Dodwell

TEN

The next morning the skies were looking bleak again. Finn made an executive decision that our treasure hunting in the Gulf was on hold 'til hurricane season passed. The forecast was not good this year.

We'd hopscotch *Time Voyager* back to the Keys, keeping close to shore and keeping a sharp eye on the weather. Once back home, we'd concentrate on fundraising and shows. All of which was fine by me. I liked Sarasota a lot, but it wasn't home.

So the day was spent prepping for departure – all being well weatherwise - though Finn did receive a phone call from Mrs. Azevedo. She hoped he would understand, but she wanted to get her daughter back home to Brazil. Alana would likely need months, if not years, of therapy to get over the trauma. Of course, Finn understood.

Mrs. Azevedo went on to say that Alana had declared she wanted none of the money her grandfather had left her – she was his sole beneficiary - her instincts were that it should be distributed to the families of the four men who'd been on the treasure hunt with him. Luma Azevedo believed the monies might have to go back to the Catholic Church, assuming it was proved they came from there in the first place.

"It's a lot to think about," she'd sighed.

A very generous amount of funds were to be wired to Finn's account in payment for his services, for which we both gave thanks.

Early in the evening I sat watching TV with Shrimp on my lap. *An Affair to Remember* was playing. You know, the movie with Cary Grant and Deborah Kerr. I love that movie; probably seen it twenty times but still I always cry, so I was well-prepared with tissues and popcorn.

Finn appeared, spruced up for his date with Dixie in tan slacks and one of his signature Hawaiian shirts.

"My, you look tastier than peach pie and ice cream."

I swear he actually blushed a little so I decided to take it easy on him.

"Tell Dixie I said 'Hi,' and go have a good time."

And Finn said, "Alrighty, then."

ELEVEN

Six months later.

The plane landed with a gentle double bounce. I'd never flown first-class before but it had taken me all of five minutes to decide it was definitely the way to go, especially when the journey took 24 hours. We'd taken Quantas from Miami, with a stopover at Los Angeles and then on to Melbourne – Australia, that is – courtesy of Luma Azevedo.

She had arranged everything. A car was at the airport to meet us and we were driven in regal style to the Queenscliff Hotel, an absolutely marvelous old Victorian establishment that, at first glance, made me think of an overly ornate wedding cake. Here, we were to spend a couple of days, resting after the long journey and finalizing our plans.

When Mrs. Azevedo had contacted Finn about this expedition it had taken him a little time to agree to it. She wanted, she said, definitive proof that the Treasure of Lima had been on the rock island where her father had been stranded. Reasonably, Finn had explained that such proof may not exist, but if she was willing to deal with potential disappointment, he was willing to take on the challenge.

The treasure hunting side of the arrangements had been left to Finn, with a seemingly unlimited budget. He had decided the best way to reach our final destination would be via Flinders Island, a ruggedly beautiful place with a rather dark history and a lot of shipwrecks. We would fly to Flinders where a boat and an experienced team of divers were at our service. The rock island's coordinates were known. They'd been well-documented when Obotien and his fellow survivors had been rescued but it would still take us upwards of eight hours to get there from Flinders.

Once we reached the rocky outcrop, Finn and three of the crew took the inflatable over. They wandered the island, which took them all of a few minutes, and found nothing. Back in the inflatable they very slowly went around the rock, poking below the waterline for evidence of a submerged cave. And they found one. Finn and two of the guys donned their gear and slipped over the side. Finn was going to explore the cave, the other men were carrying electrical devices to repel any possible shark attacks. They'd been lectured by Finn, however, that they were only to be used if there was imminent danger.

I was a bundle of nerves while Finn was out of sight. I spotted a couple of sharks near the surface, so I knew there would be more around, and I wasn't nearly as sure as he was that sharks aren't particularly interested in us. I mean, they attacked the one treasure hunter who tried to swim from here.

When I saw all three men reappear I was hugely relieved. They continued around the whole island but found nothing else.

"Well?" I queried Finn when he was back on board. He merely shook his head.

"Mrs Azevedo will be disappointed," I said.

"Maybe not."

Now what did he mean by that?

We were back at the Queenscliff Hotel for a night. Our flight was due to leave the next day and we were making the most of beer-battered King George whiting and chips in a corner of the Boat Bar. It was especially delicious with a glass of local brew.

I popped a morsel in my mouth. "Shrimp would love this fish."

"I'm sure she's been very well fed."

Time Voyager was at Stock Island in the Florida Keys and Shrimp was being watched over by the neighboring shrimpers.

"As much as I could get used to this life, I miss Shrimp, and nothing quite beats living aboard *Time Voyager*. I just wish we had some good news for Luma and Alena."

"Who said we don't?"

Frowning I looked suspiciously at Finn. "Give."

With exaggerated care he reached in his pocket and pulled out a small pouch. "Don't let anyone see it," he said.

Wordlessly, I upended the pouch over my open hand and an intense, radiant green stone fell into it. An emerald. I looked at Finn and he gave me back a look that just said 'Yep.'

"It was all real." I didn't know what else to say, so I clutched the jewel and started laughing. Only Finn could dive into an underwater cave in shark-infested waters and manage to find one tiny stone. Amazing.

"I think we'd better order another round," said Finn.

The End

Become part of the In-crowd and get a FREE short story:

http://lizdodwell.com/signup/

Find all of Liz's books here.

http://lizdodwell.com/books/

Liz Dodwell

Author's Notes

So, you're probably wondering if the Treasure of Lima really exists. Well, maybe.

The general consensus is that William Thompson stole the treasure and buried it on Cocos Island. Over the years, before Cocos became a UNESCO (*United Nations Educational, Scientific and Cultural Organization*) World Heritage Site, a good number of treasure seekers dug around the island without success. Then there was August Gissler, a German, who spent 19 years living on the island hunting the treasure but found only six gold coins.

Interestingly, in 2012 UNESCO granted permission to a British explorer to search for the treasure. However, whether the project is ongoing or not, I don't know.

The name Benito "Bloody Sword" Bonito cropped up variously in my research as Captain Thompson's mate; a Portuguese pirate who buried treasure on Cocos that was unrelated to that of Lima; and the pirate who stole the Lima loot and hid it at Queenscliff, Australia.

One inventory of the treasure supposedly lists 113 gold religious statues, including a life-size Virgin Mary; 200 chests of jewels; 273 swords with jeweled hilts; 1,000 diamonds; solid gold crowns; 150 chalices; and hundreds of gold and silver bars.

Liz Dodwell

As with so many lost treasures, the story is shrouded in myth and mystery.

Some of you will realize I have taken inspiration for the character of Finn from real-life treasure hunter, Captain Carl Fismer. Carl, or 'Fizz' as many people know him, has been a good friend for many years. Not only is he one of the most interesting people I know he's also one of the nicest, and I owe him a big 'thank you' for his input and guidance. Find out more about him on his website: http://www.carlfismer.com/

A big thanks also to my multi-talented assistant, Dominic Ottaviano, who not only keeps my computer network running smoothly but does everything else from video to formatting, research, book cover design...you name it. And special thanks to my biggest fan who always believes in me, my husband, Alex Markovich.

Most of all, I want to thank you, my readers. You know, as an independent author it's not easy to compete with the big guys. So if you liked *The Mystery of the One-Armed Man*, I would really appreciate if you'd take a few moments to leave a review.

By the way, you can also be among the first to know about new books, special deals and advance review copies, when you join my email list here:

http://lizdodwell.com/signup

Captain Finn Treasure Mysteries is on ongoing series, though each book contains an individual story.

Get the next book:

http://lizdodwell.com/signup/

Liz Dodwell

Black Bart is Dead

Here's an excerpt from the second book in the Captain Finn treasure mystery series.

ONE

Calico Jack had sipped a little too much grog. The overly bright eyes, flushed cheeks and raised voice were enough of a giveaway without Anne Bonny, one hand on hip, the other on the hilt of her sword, telling him in a hissed whisper to 'Sober up!'

Frankly, I found it rather amusing. After all, we were pirates – at least for the night – weren't we supposed to be a bunch of rum-swigging, dissolute ruffians?

Perhaps I'd better explain. Finn and I were guests at a pirate murder mystery dinner on Mud Bug Island, the private hideaway of Elbert Lex Van Nifterik, who goes by Bert. There were 10 of us, plus the butler and maid, all decked out in appropriate pirate garb and punctuating our speech with lots of 'aye ayes' and 'aarghs.'

It all began with SAV. That's an acronym for *Service Animals for Vets* - pronounced SAVE - a charitable organization that rescues animals from shelters and trains them as guide dogs, mobility assistance dogs and hearing assistance dogs for disabled military veterans. It's a great concept; people rescue animals and in return the animals rescue people.

Finn had been the guest speaker at a recent fundraising event for SAV. The other star of the show was a beautiful black labrador, Luna, who had been rescued from a high-kill shelter the day before she was scheduled to be put down. Now she was in training with a local foster family. Anyway, that was when we met Bert.

At just 12 years of age, Bert was designing – and selling - video games, most of them with a pirate theme. At 17 he speculated by buying bitcoin, a virtual currency, when it was only one dollar. He sold it later for $6000 apiece. Not surprisingly, now in his mid-20s, Bert is worth millions.

The organizer of the event was Delia Beaton Baynes, otherwise known as Dilly. The minute she opened her mouth I started thinking of her as Silly Dilly. She was a good-looking woman, well put together, with the intellect of a jellyfish and the tentacles to match. She was all over Finn, clinging to him tighter than a limpet to a rock. Not that it's unusual for women to be drawn to Finn. He's a guy you might say is ruggedly handsome, but his real attraction is that he genuinely likes women. He listens to them and he appreciates them. In Dilly's case, though, she was after someone she thought had money and status.

Finn is a shipwreck treasure hunter. That's what his talks are about. His full name is Rex Finsmer but nobody ever calls him Rex; it's always Finn or Captain Finn. I'm Phillida Jane Trent – you can call me Phill – and I work with Finn. I also live on his boat, *Time Voyager*, with him. Although we're not related, he's like a father to me. In fact, he's the only family I have.

At the SAV event we'd set up a display of treasures, many of which were for sale, the proceeds going to the charity. Bert had purchased several high ticket items, and spent some time chatting with Finn. Seems he was quite enamored of pirates and treasure hunting and had come to the event specifically to meet Finn. When Dilly realized Bert was the wealthy recluse of Mud Bug Island fame, she immediately pounced on him, insisting he host another event. He did his best to decline, but was no match for Dilly. And when she came up with the idea of a pirate mystery dinner, he agreed to it on condition that Finn was in attendance.

So here we were. Finn as himself, in the pirate costume he wore for his visits to the Children's Hospital, where he was known as 'the kids' favorite pirate.' I'd decided to go as Anne Dieu-le-Veut. In 1683, her buccaneer husband was killed by another pirate, Laurens de Graff, in a bar fight. To avenge her husband's death Anne challenged Laurens to a duel. Laurens refused to fight a woman but promptly proposed to her instead. From then on they lived as husband and wife and commanded their pirate ship together. When Laurens was later killed, Anne took his place as Captain. She seemed like a woman I would have liked. *Just saying.*

We were gathered in the great room of Bert's island home, waiting for the game to begin. Originally, Bert had planned to hold the event on his yacht, but weather got in the way of that. Tropical storm Darla was being spiteful, and threatening to claw her way around the Keys, so Bert came in his launch to pick us up from the mainland. The mood had been light-hearted as we waited at the public dock, decked out in our pirate duds. Tourists gawped at us and we gave them a show of pistol-toting, saber-waving bluster until Bert, as Barbarossa, the fierce 16th century Barbary pirate, pulled alongside yelling 'Avast, me hearties!'

One young woman had kept herself apart from the rest of us. An elfin little thing, looking awkward and shy in her wench's costume. I'd introduced myself and she told me her name was Teresa and that she had been hired to assist for the evening as a maid. I tried to draw her into conversation but her every response to my comments was monosyllabic, so I decided to leave her to herself.

Mud Bug is less than six miles offshore and a 20 minute boat ride. There's a natural horseshoe-shaped basin on the east side with extensive dockage. Monks, who is Bert's English butler-cum-factotum was there to greet us and help tie up. He was the only other person on the island, and once we were ashore, he led us into the main house. It wasn't what I expected; especially for a young guy. The walls were white, presumably in deference to the warm climate, and the style of the home modern, but the woodwork and wood flooring were in variegated tones of sunflower blond to rich cocoa and had an aged quality to them. Patterned rugs in Dresden blue and white were scattered around and the furniture was an eclectic mix of Chippendale, Victorian and Louis XVI. Not that I'm any expert, mind you, but I've watched my share of *Antiques Road Show* episodes.

"The flooring and the doors are reclaimed chestnut wood from a monastery in Tuscany."

I hadn't noticed Bert come up behind me. "You brought wood all the way from Italy?"

"Why not? It's beautiful. I thought it deserved to be showcased, rather than chopped up for firewood."

Couldn't argue with that.

"Would you care for a Mud Bug Special, madam?" I heard Monks speak and looked around to see who he was addressing before I realized it was me. *Madam?* That made me feel almost as old as the monastery doors.

I eyed the drinks tray he held out. "There are wormy-looking things that seem to be trying to escape from the glasses."

"Yes, madam. Gummy worms soaked in dark rum. A little black food coloring is added to the rum so the worms take on a more natural 'buggy' appearance."

OK, now I was officially interested. "And what's in the muddy concoction?"

"Spiced rum, Amarula cream, Kahlua, Canton ginger liqueur and fresh lime juice."

"Sounds a bit on the sweet side for a pre-dinner beverage."

"I think, madam, you will find the tartness of the lime and the quantity of spiced rum will balance out the sweetness."

And indeed I did. The drink was delicious, and boozy gummy worms might be one of my new favorite things.

"Why Blackbeard?"

"Madam?"

"You are Blackbeard, aren't you?" I eyeballed the coils of black facial hair and the daggers and pistols stuffed into sashes crisscrossing his chest.

"Quite so. It seemed appropriate to play the part of another Englishman, and Edward Teach – that's Blackbeard's real name – and I have something more in common: we both come from the port town of Bristol. Now, if you will excuse me…" And in a very un-Blackbeard-like manner, Monks gracefully eased himself away, leaving me with Bert.

"I think that dreadful woman," Bert lifted his chin in Dilly's direction, "is after Finn. Should we help him?"

I followed his gaze and watched Dilly leading Finn round like a prize heifer – or should I say bull? – introducing him to the others with an air of 'he's mine, don't touch him.'

"Nah. He can take care of himself." Secretly, I was enjoying his discomfort. "She's just an over-sexed vixen."

"There's more to it than that."

"Why monsieur," I affected my best French piratess accent, "do tell."

"According to my sources.…" I gave Bert one of those 'get real' looks. "Oh, alright. According to Monks – he gets all the local dirt from Wicked Wally's tavern on the mainland – Dilly was married to a man 30 years her senior. When he died he had certain provisos in his will that ensured her, shall we say, constancy."

"So he bribed her."

"Well, yes. I suppose you could call it that. She has a lifetime interest in their home and a reasonable allowance, provided she raises a minimum $100,000 a year for hubby's favorite charity, SAV."

"Wow. That's a bit stiff. But can't she just put some of her allowance towards it? "

"Apparently not. And, of course, if she remarries, she loses everything and has to pay back whatever allowance she's received to date."

"Surely that can't be legal?"

"Her husband was a judge, so he should know."

"The judge was a mean old bastard! I actually feel a little sorry for her. No wonder she's all over Finn. She needs a rich new husband as soon as possible to get her out of this before she's in too deep. Perhaps I should warn him."

Before I had a chance to do so, the sound of a gong crashed through the room, followed by Monks' monotone voice, "Dinner is served."

Liz Dodwell …was told so many times

that she really knew how to spin a yarn, she finally decided to put that talent to good use. Taking inspiration from her good friend and real-life treasure hunter, Captain Carl Fismer, she created the Captain Finn Treasure Mystery series.

For several years Liz worked with the Captain, operating his website and arranging talks and treasure exhibitions. "I would dive when I got the chance, but only on a hookah," she says. "I never found anything of real importance, but just knowing I was getting even a microscopic glimpse of history and adventure was truly exciting."

Fueled by an occasional cup of grog, Liz writes from the home she shares with husband Alex and a crew of rescued dogs and cats. For a change of pace she pens stories in cozy mystery and romantic suspense. For relaxation she likes to yodel. (Just kidding).

www.LizDodwell.com